We Love Bunk Beds!

Paula Metcalf

Macmillan Children's Books

For my big sister, Maripi

First published 2007 by Macmillan Children's Books
a division of Macmillan Publishers Limited
20 New Wharf Road, London N1 9RR
Basingstoke and Oxford
Associated companies throughout the world
www.panmacmillan.com

ISBN: 978-1-4050-4946-7 (HB)
ISBN: 978-1-4050-5565-9 (PB)

Text and illustrations copyright © Paula Metcalf 2007

Moral rights asserted

1 3 5 7 9 8 6 4 2

A CIP catalogue record for this book is available from the British Library.

Printed in China

No matter where Shirley was . . .

her little sister Doris was never far away.

Doris wanted to be with Shirley EVERYWHERE!

This was not always a good thing.

But if Mummy ever needed to find Doris,
she never had to look very far.

Shirley got so used to her little sister being around that she sometimes forgot that Doris was even there.

Shirley loved to ride her bike (and so did Doris!).

But Mummy worried that this was dangerous

so she bought the girls a present . . .

"Oh dear!"
sighed Mummy.

Shirley and Doris shared a bedroom.

Doris's side of the room was always neat and tidy.

But Shirley's wasn't! Poor Shirley, her bed
wasn't big enough for TWO growing elephants.

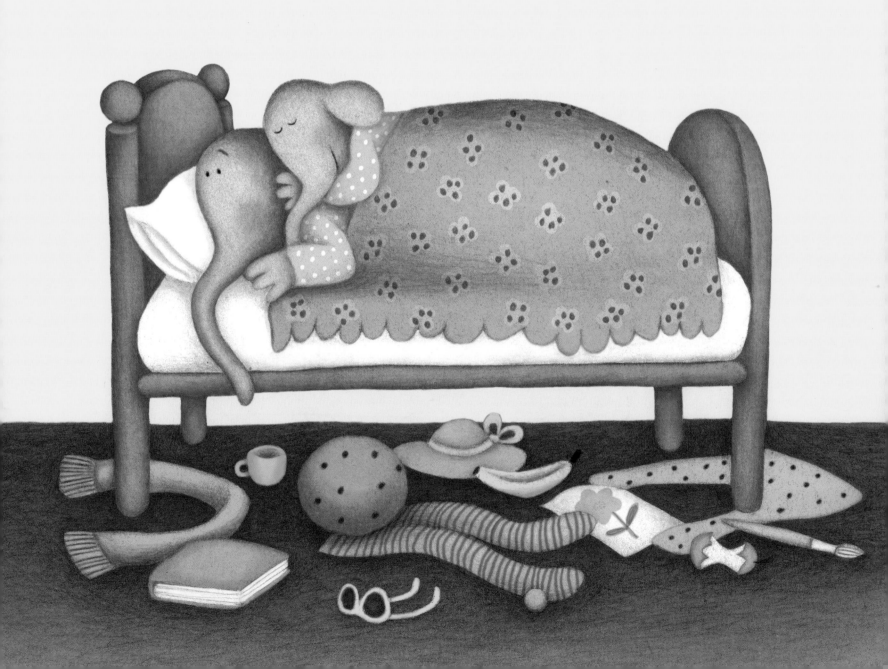

One day, Mummy said, "You're a big girl now, Doris.

Wouldn't you like to sleep in your own bed?"

Doris didn't like Mummy's idea very much.

But then Mummy had another idea.

"Everybody in the car," she called. "We're going into town."

In the furniture shop was something Doris
had never seen before – BUNK BEDS!

"If we got bunk beds, Doris," said Mummy,

"you could stay close to Shirley every night."

Luckily for everyone, Doris loved the idea. Mummy ordered

the bunk beds. They would be delivered next Tuesday.

Doris quickly became a bunk bed expert. "The best thing about bunk beds,"
she explained, "is that sometimes you can sleep on the top,
and sometimes you can sleep on the bottom."

"Exactly," said Shirley, "we can even swap
over every night if you like!"

"Hooray," shouted Doris, "I can't wait!"

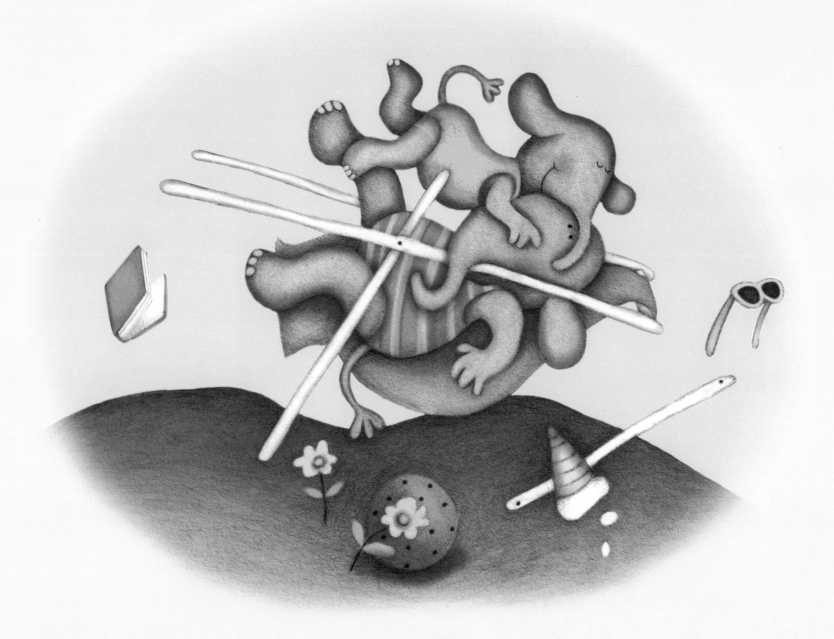

Neither could Shirley.

Finally the bunk beds arrived.
"Top or bottom, Shirley?" asked Doris
at bedtime. Shirley couldn't believe her luck.
She clambered up to the top bunk.

"Good idea, Shirley,"

said Doris . . .

. . . and tomorrow we'll sleep on the bottom!"